MOON GIRL AND DEVIL DINOSAUR

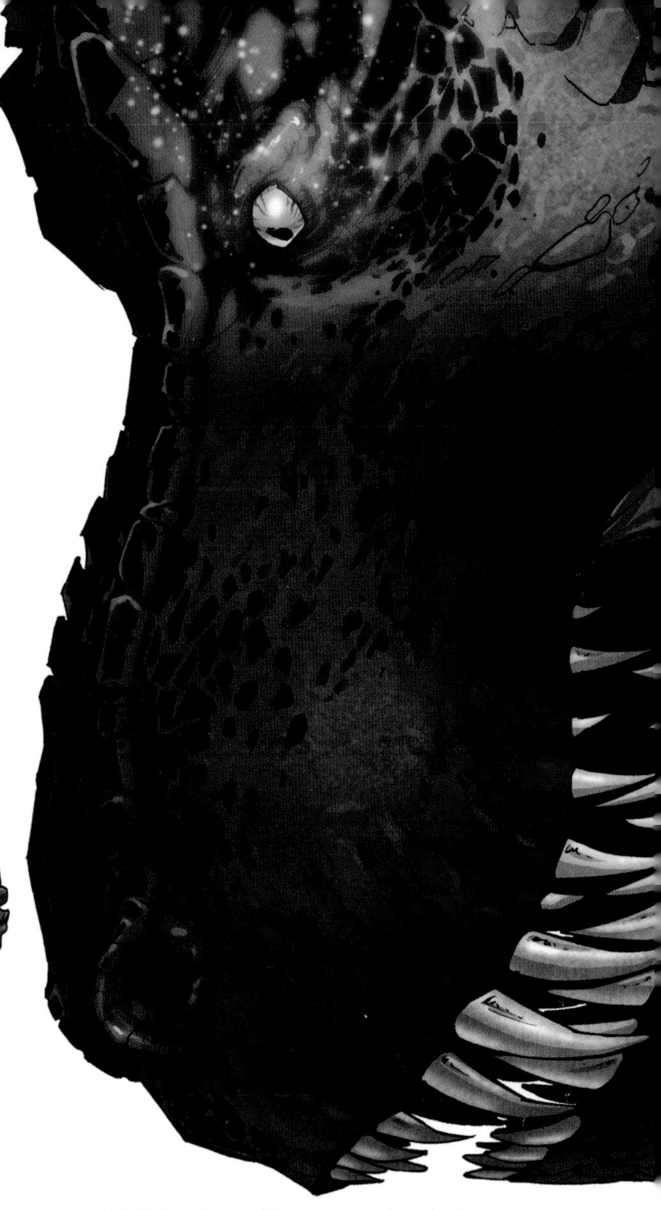

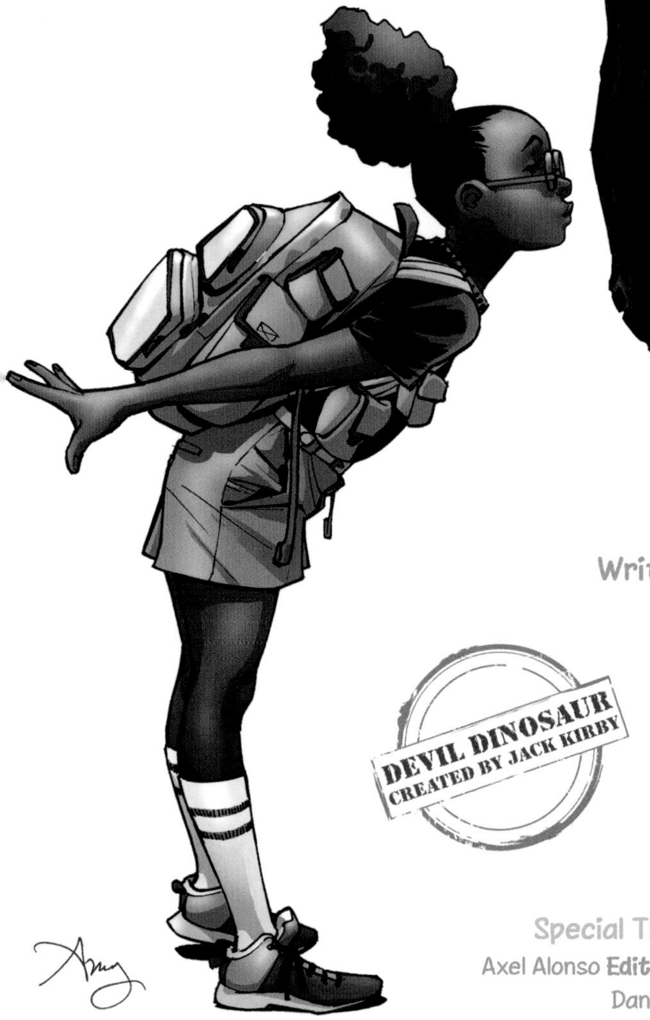

BFF #1: Repeat After Me

Writers: Brandon Montclare & Amy Reeder
Artist: Natacha Bustos
Colorist: Tamra Bonvillain
Letterer: VC's Travis Lanham
Production Design: Manny Mederos
Editors: Mark Paniccia & Emily Shaw
Cover: Amy Reeder
Variant Cover: Trevor Von Eeden
Hip Hop Variant: Jeffrey Veregge

DEVIL DINOSAUR CREATED BY JACK KIRBY

Special Thanks to Sana Amanat and David Gabriel

Axel Alonso **Editor in Chief** Joe Quesada **Chief Creative Officer**
Dan Buckley **Publisher** Alan Fine **Executive Producer**

MARVEL
marvelkids.com

ABDO Spotlight

ABDOPUBLISHING.COM

Reinforced library bound edition published in 2018 by Spotlight,
a division of ABDO, PO Box 398166, Minneapolis, Minnesota 55439.
Spotlight produces high-quality reinforced library bound editions for
schools and libraries. Published by agreement with Marvel Characters, Inc.

Printed in the United States of America, North Mankato, Minnesota.
042017
092017

THIS BOOK CONTAINS
RECYCLED MATERIALS

marvelkids.com
© 2017 MARVEL

PUBLISHER'S CATALOGING IN PUBLICATION DATA

Names: Reeder, Amy ; Montclare, Brandon, authors. | Bustos, Natacha ; Bonvillain,
    Tamra, illustrators.
Title: Repeat after me / writers: Amy Reeder ; Brandon Montclare ; art: Natacha
    Bustos ; Tamra Bonvillain.
Description: Reinforced library bound edition. | Minneapolis, Minnesota : Spotlight,
    2018. | Series: Moon Girl and Devil Dinosaur ; BFF #1
Summary: Lunella can't wait to study the Omni-Wave Projector she found, but
    when it's activated during gym class, it creates a time portal, bringing forth the
    Devil Dinosaur, along with the evil Killer Folk, who still stop at nothing to claim
    the device for themselves.
Identifiers: LCCN 2016961924 | ISBN 9781532140082 (lib. bdg.)
Subjects: LCSH: Schools--Juvenile fiction. | Adventure and adventurers--Juvenile
    fiction. | Comic Books, strips, etc.--Juvenile fiction. | Graphic novels Juvenile
    fiction.
Classification: DDC 741.5--dc23
LC record available at https://lccn.loc.gov/2016961924

Spotlight

A Division of ABDO
abdopublishing.com

"Humanity is leaving its childhood and moving into its adolescence as its powers infuse into a realm hitherto beyond our reach." - Dr. Gregory Stock

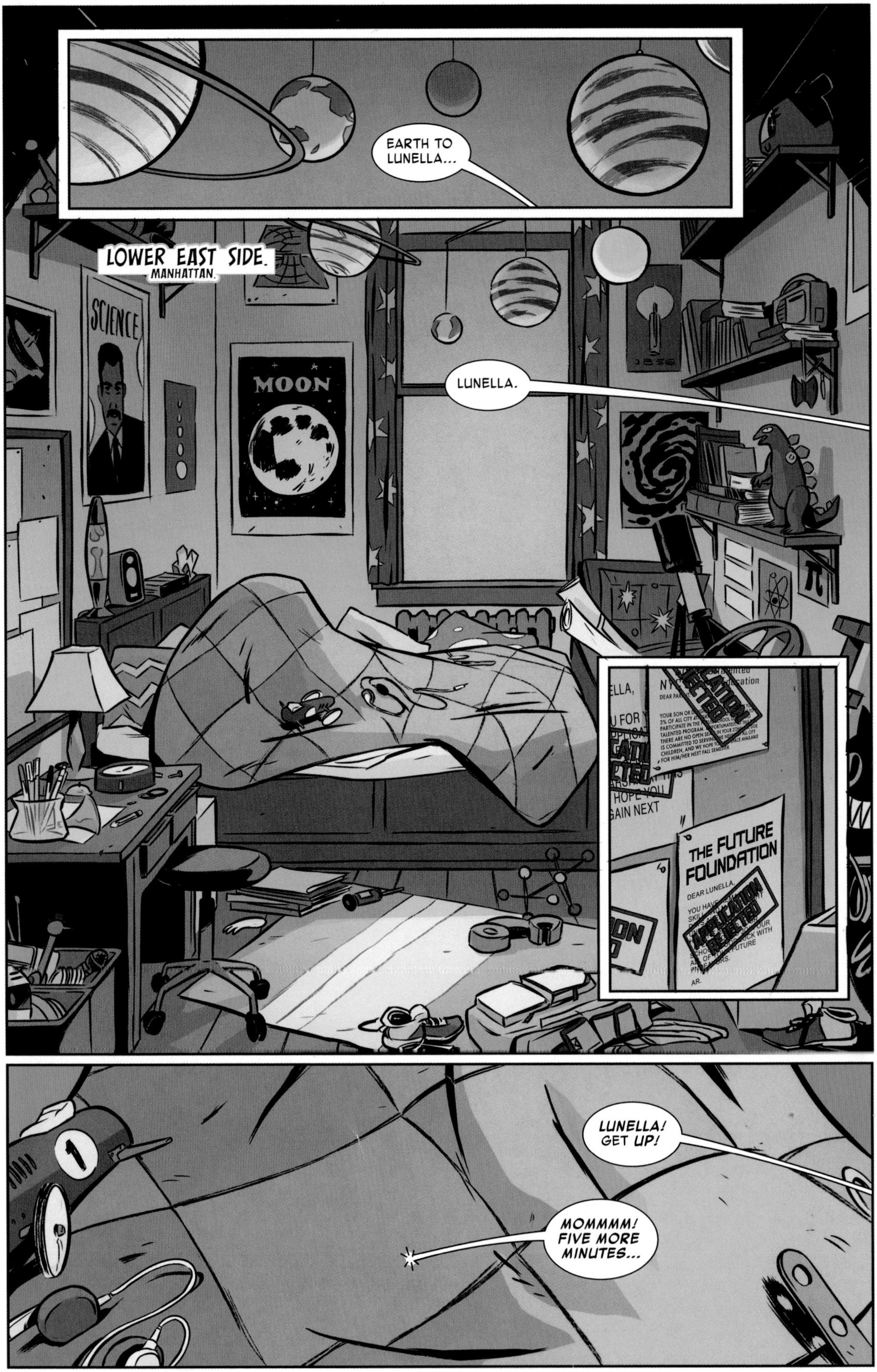
EARTH TO LUNELLA...
LOWER EAST SIDE.
MANHATTAN.
SCIENCE
MOON
LUNELLA.
THE FUTURE FOUNDATION
DEAR LUNELLA,
APPLICATION REJECTED
LUNELLA! GET UP!
MOMMMM! FIVE MORE MINUTES...

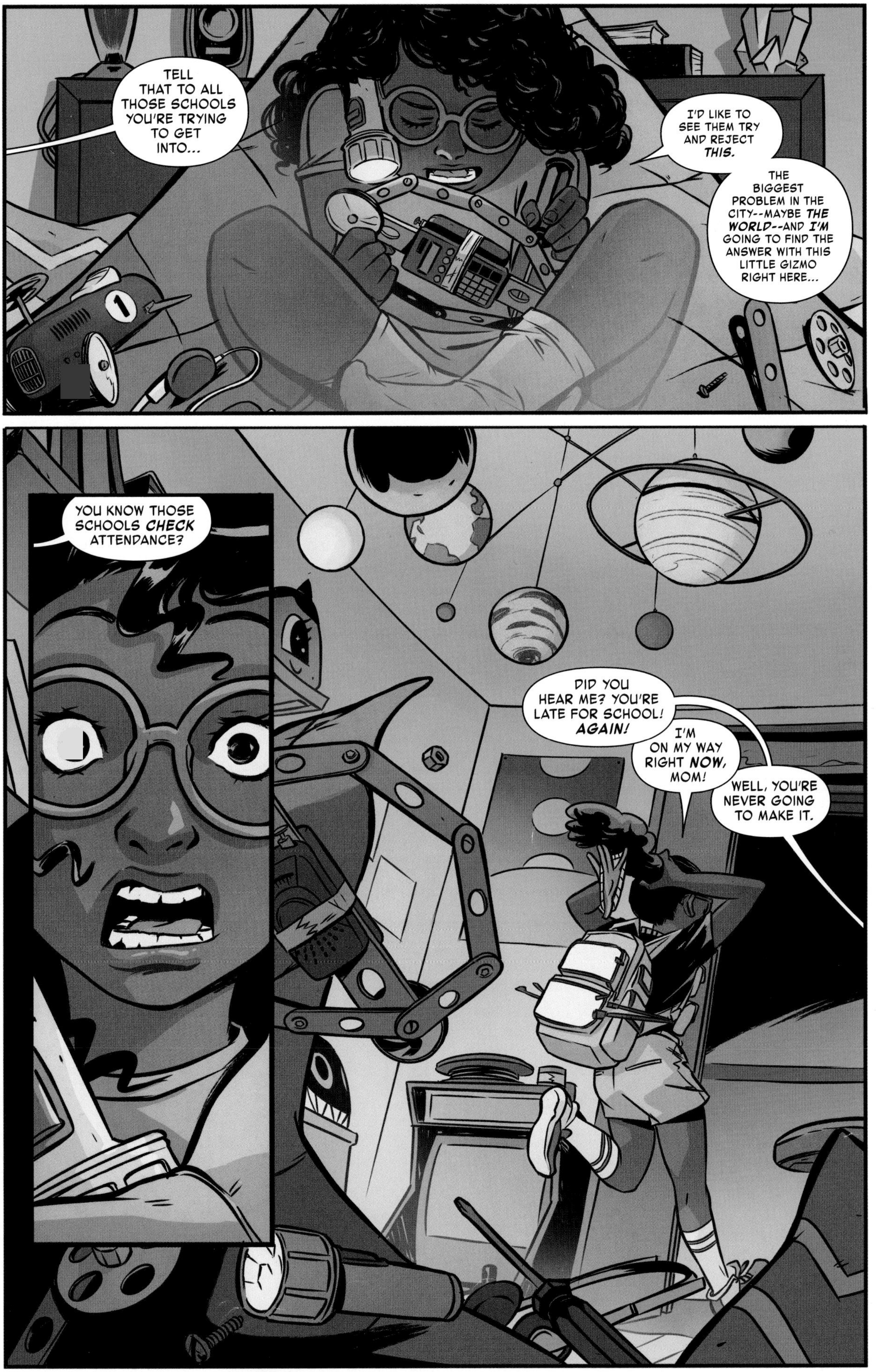
TELL THAT TO ALL THOSE SCHOOLS YOU'RE TRYING TO GET INTO...
I'D LIKE TO SEE THEM TRY AND REJECT *THIS.*
THE BIGGEST PROBLEM IN THE CITY--MAYBE *THE WORLD*--AND *I'M* GOING TO FIND THE ANSWER WITH THIS LITTLE GIZMO RIGHT HERE...
YOU KNOW THOSE SCHOOLS *CHECK* ATTENDANCE?
DID YOU HEAR ME? YOU'RE LATE FOR SCHOOL! *AGAIN!*
I'M ON MY WAY RIGHT *NOW,* MOM!
WELL, YOU'RE NEVER GOING TO MAKE IT.

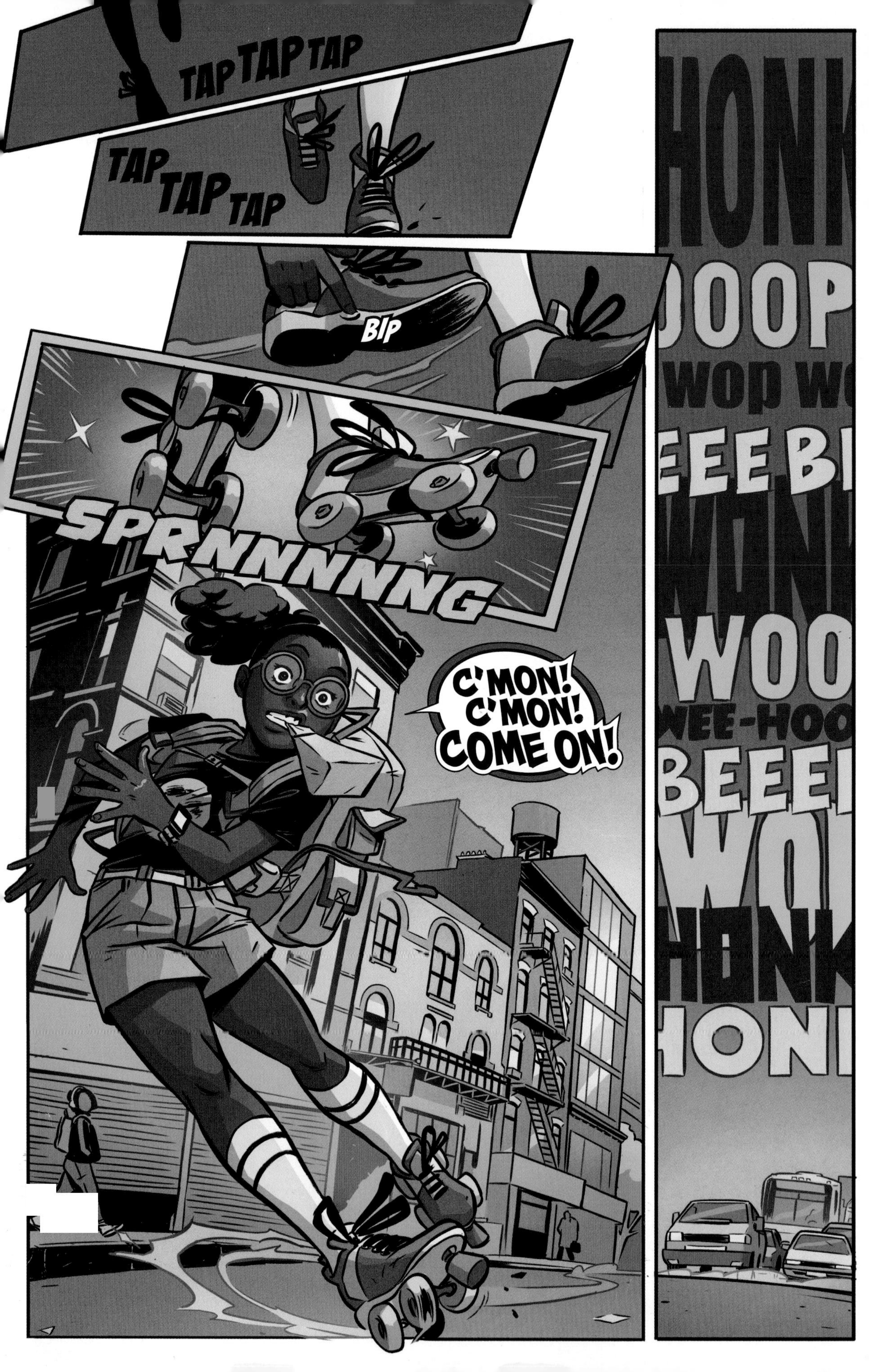
TAP TAP TAP
TAP TAP TAP
BIP
SPRNNNNNNG
C'MON! C'MON! COME ON!
HONK
OOOP
wop w
EEEB
WOO
WEE-HOO
BEEE
HONK
HON

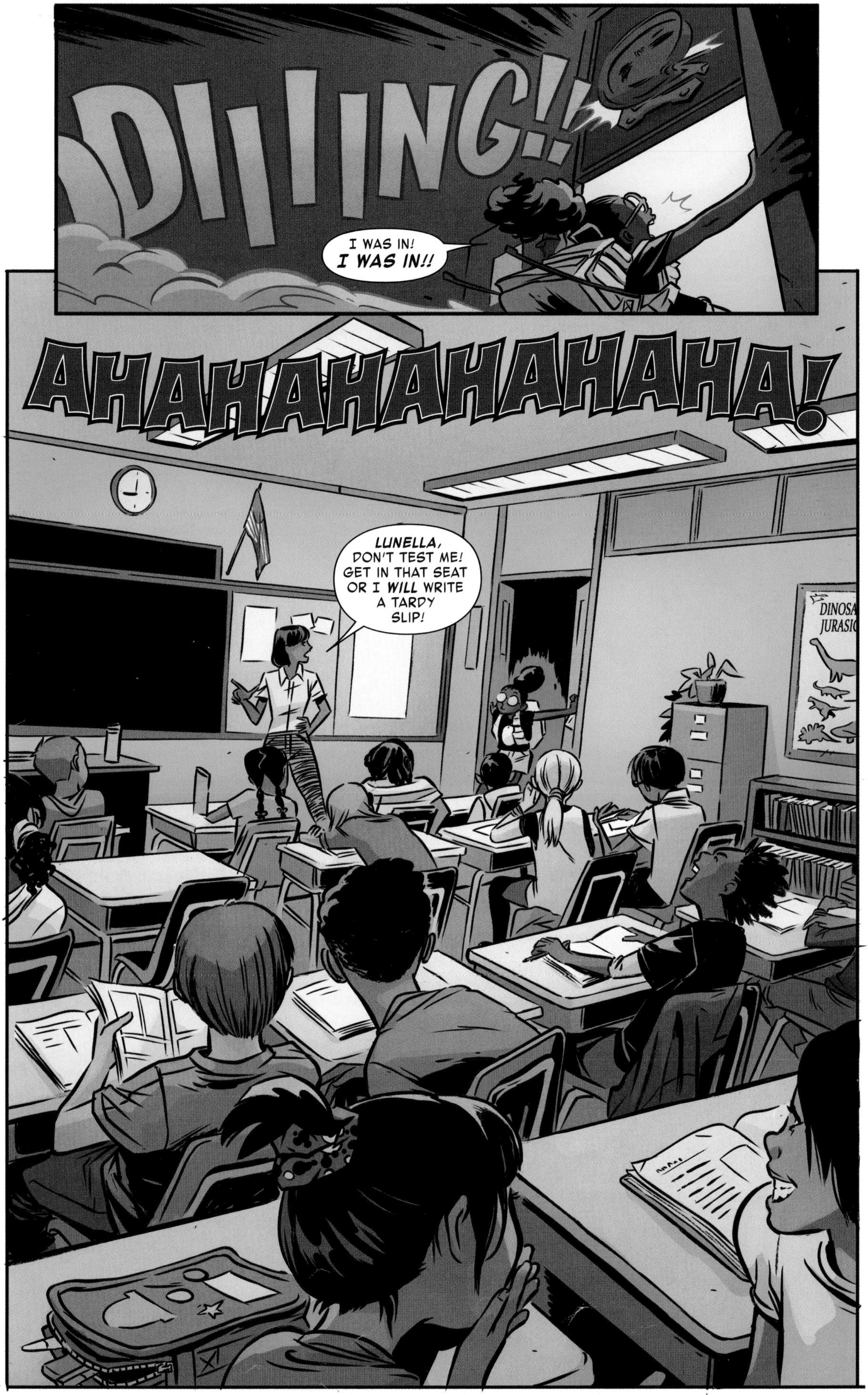
DIIIING!!
I WAS IN!
I WAS IN!!
AHAHAHAHAHAHAHA!
LUNELLA, DON'T TEST ME! GET IN THAT SEAT OR I WILL WRITE A TARDY SLIP!

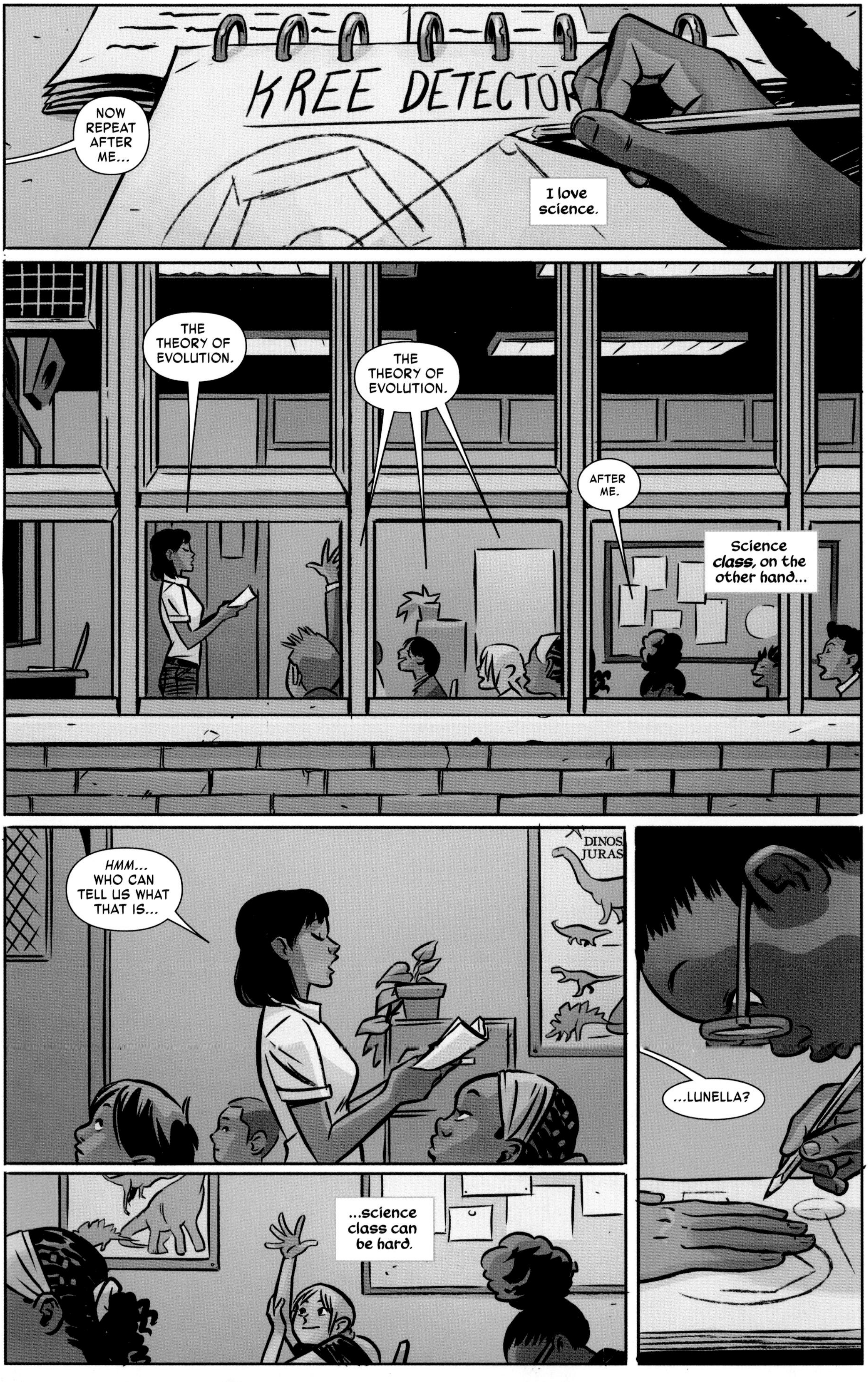
KREE DETECTOR
NOW REPEAT AFTER ME...
I love science.
THE THEORY OF EVOLUTION.
THE THEORY OF EVOLUTION.
AFTER ME.
Science *class,* on the other hand...
HMM... WHO CAN TELL US WHAT THAT IS...
...LUNELLA?
...science class can be hard.

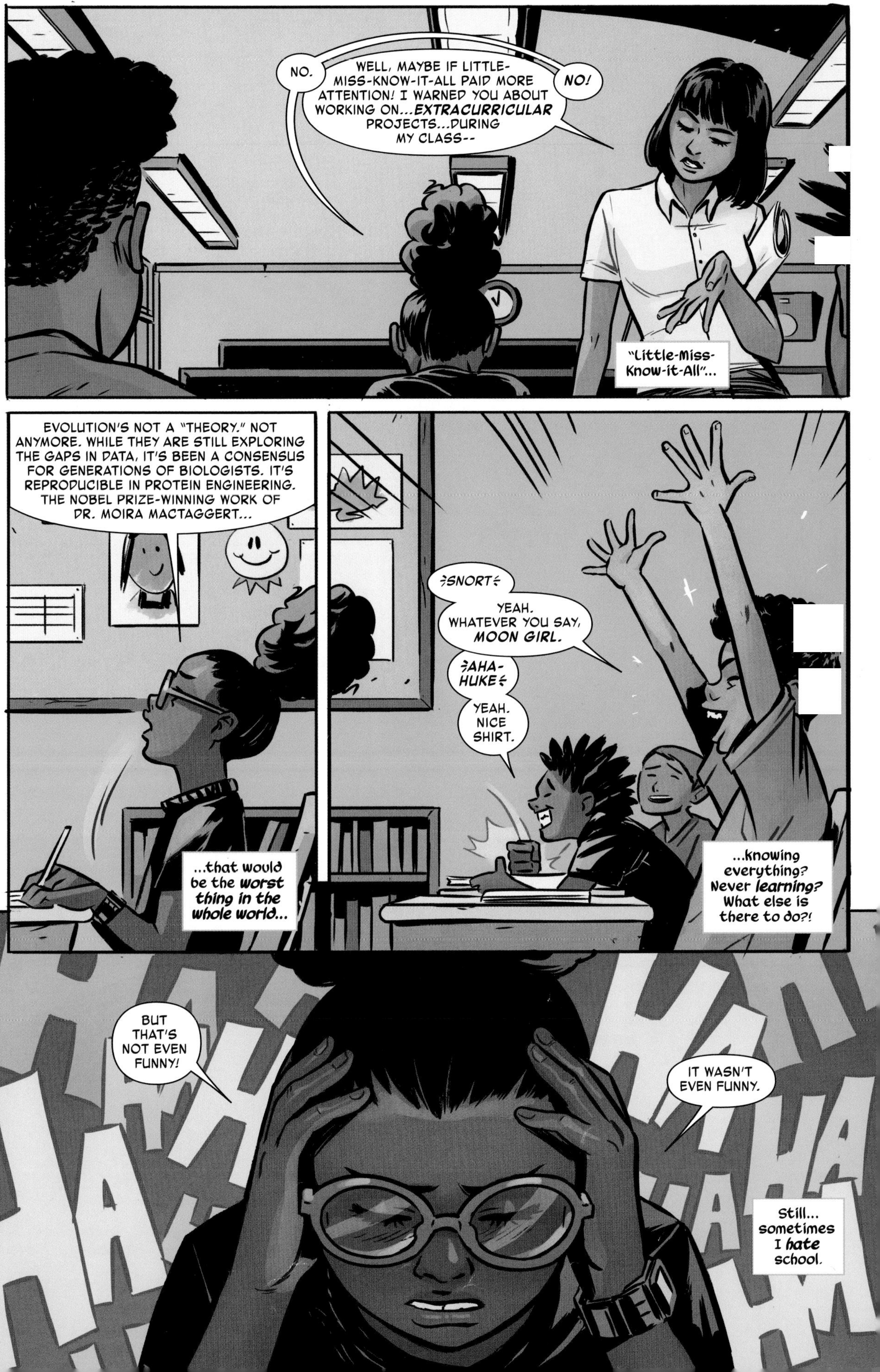
NO.
WELL, MAYBE IF LITTLE-MISS-KNOW-IT-ALL PAID MORE ATTENTION! I WARNED YOU ABOUT WORKING ON...EXTRACURRICULAR PROJECTS...DURING MY CLASS--
NO!
"Little-Miss-Know-it-All"...
EVOLUTION'S NOT A "THEORY." NOT ANYMORE. WHILE THEY ARE STILL EXPLORING THE GAPS IN DATA, IT'S BEEN A CONSENSUS FOR GENERATIONS OF BIOLOGISTS. IT'S REPRODUCIBLE IN PROTEIN ENGINEERING. THE NOBEL PRIZE-WINNING WORK OF DR. MOIRA MACTAGGERT...
...that would be the worst thing in the whole world...
SNORT
YEAH. WHATEVER YOU SAY, MOON GIRL.
AHA-HUKE
YEAH. NICE SHIRT.
...knowing everything? Never learning? What else is there to do?!
BUT THAT'S NOT EVEN FUNNY!
IT WASN'T EVEN FUNNY.
Still... sometimes I hate school.

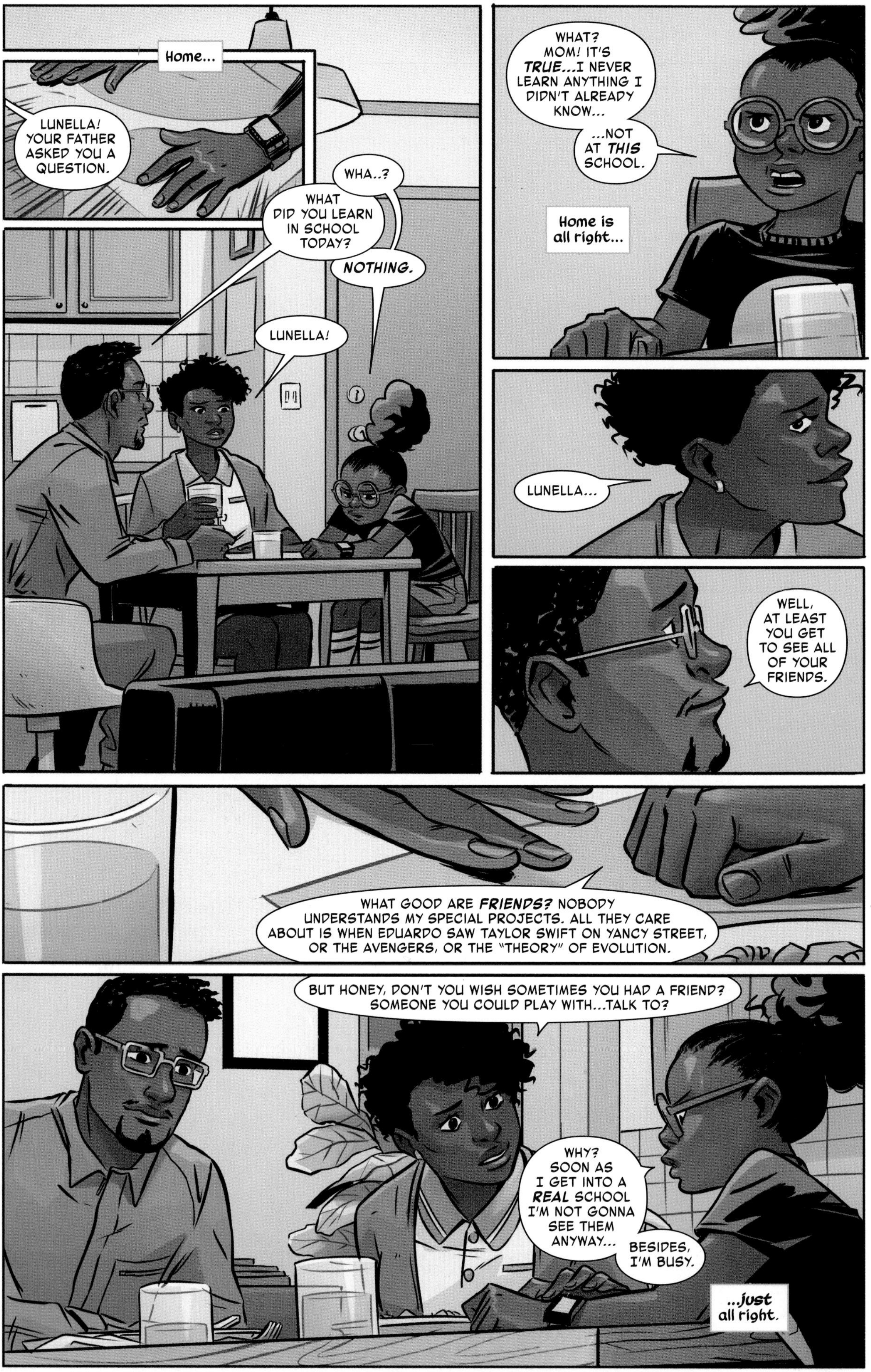
Home...
LUNELLA! YOUR FATHER ASKED YOU A QUESTION.
WHAT? MOM! IT'S TRUE...I NEVER LEARN ANYTHING I DIDN'T ALREADY KNOW...
...NOT AT THIS SCHOOL.
Home is all right...
WHA..?
WHAT DID YOU LEARN IN SCHOOL TODAY?
NOTHING.
LUNELLA!
LUNELLA...
WELL, AT LEAST YOU GET TO SEE ALL OF YOUR FRIENDS.
WHAT GOOD ARE FRIENDS? NOBODY UNDERSTANDS MY SPECIAL PROJECTS. ALL THEY CARE ABOUT IS WHEN EDUARDO SAW TAYLOR SWIFT ON YANCY STREET, OR THE AVENGERS, OR THE "THEORY" OF EVOLUTION.
BUT HONEY, DON'T YOU WISH SOMETIMES YOU HAD A FRIEND? SOMEONE YOU COULD PLAY WITH...TALK TO?
WHY? SOON AS I GET INTO A REAL SCHOOL I'M NOT GONNA SEE THEM ANYWAY...
BESIDES, I'M BUSY.
...just all right.

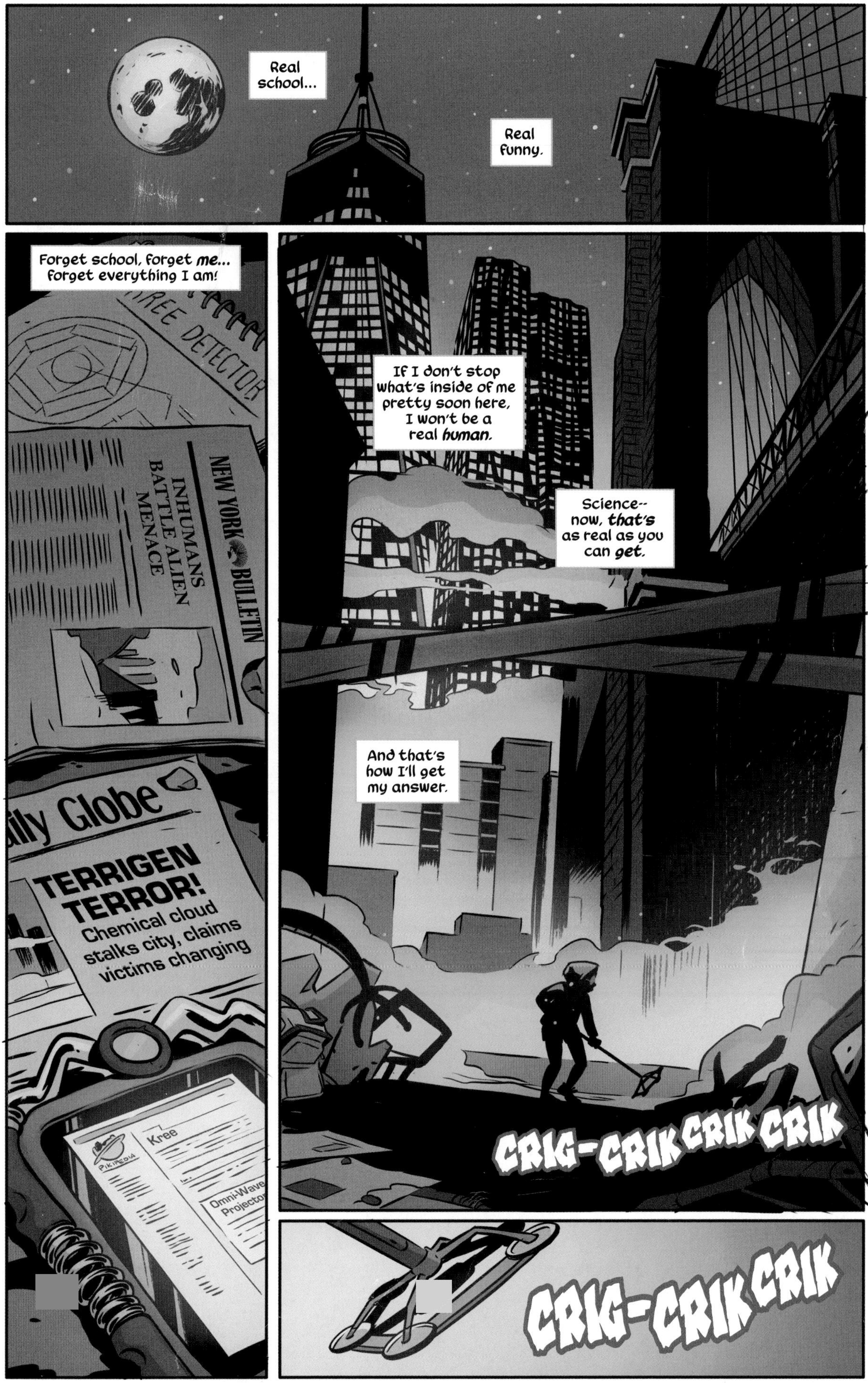

Real school...
Real funny.
Forget school, forget *me*... forget everything I am!
KREE DETECTOR
NEW YORK BULLETIN
INHUMANS BATTLE ALIEN MENACE
ily Globe
TERRIGEN TERROR!
Chemical cloud stalks city, claims victims changing
PIKIPEDIA
Kree
Omni-Wave Projector
If I don't stop what's inside of me pretty soon here, I won't be a real *human.*
Science--now, *that's* as real as you can *get.*
And that's how I'll get my answer.
CRIG-CRIK CRIK CRIK
CRIG-CRIK CRIK

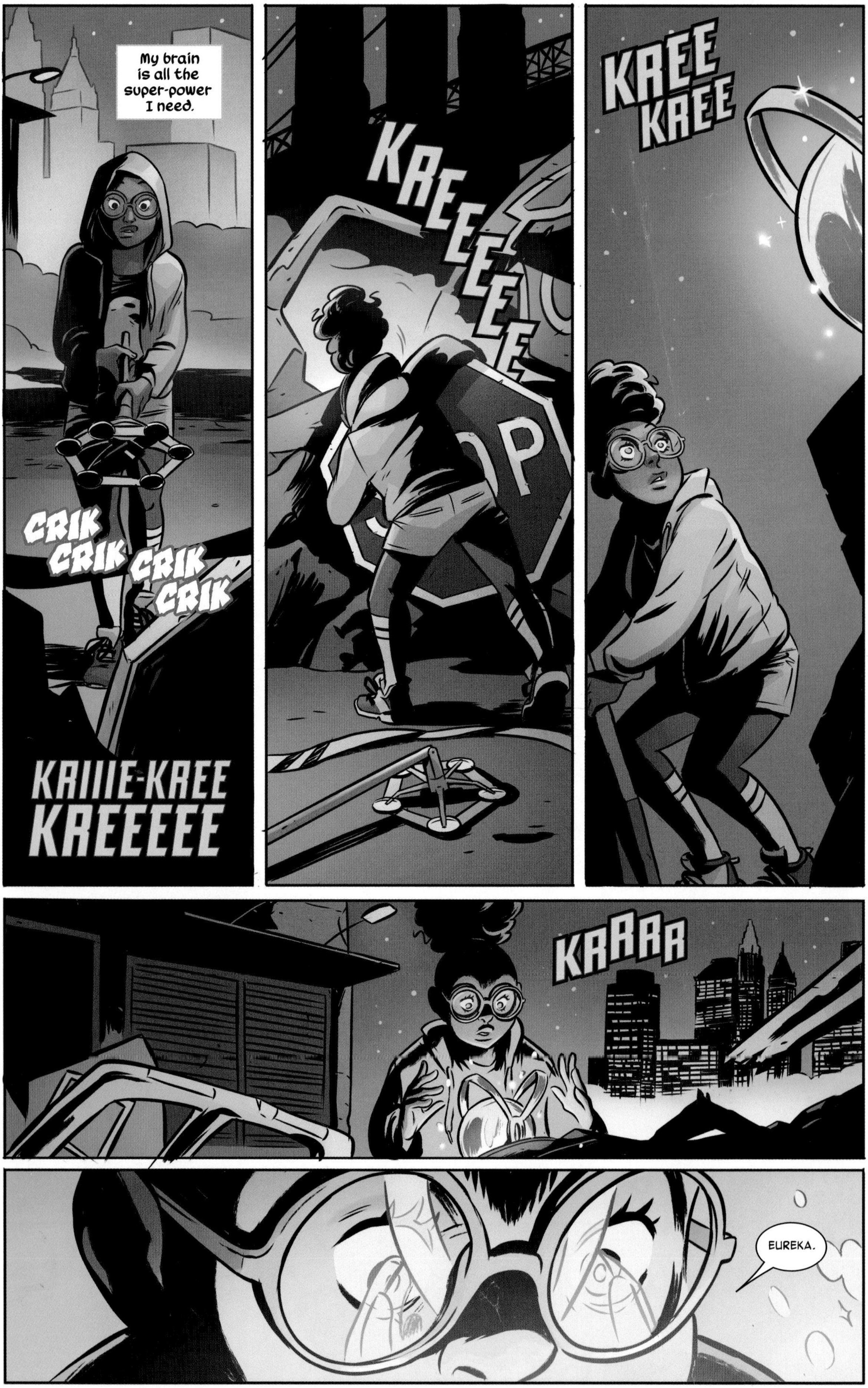
My brain is all the super-power I need.
CRIK CRIK CRIK CRIK
KRIIIE-KREE KREEEEE
KREEEEEE
KREE KREE
KRRRR
EUREKA.

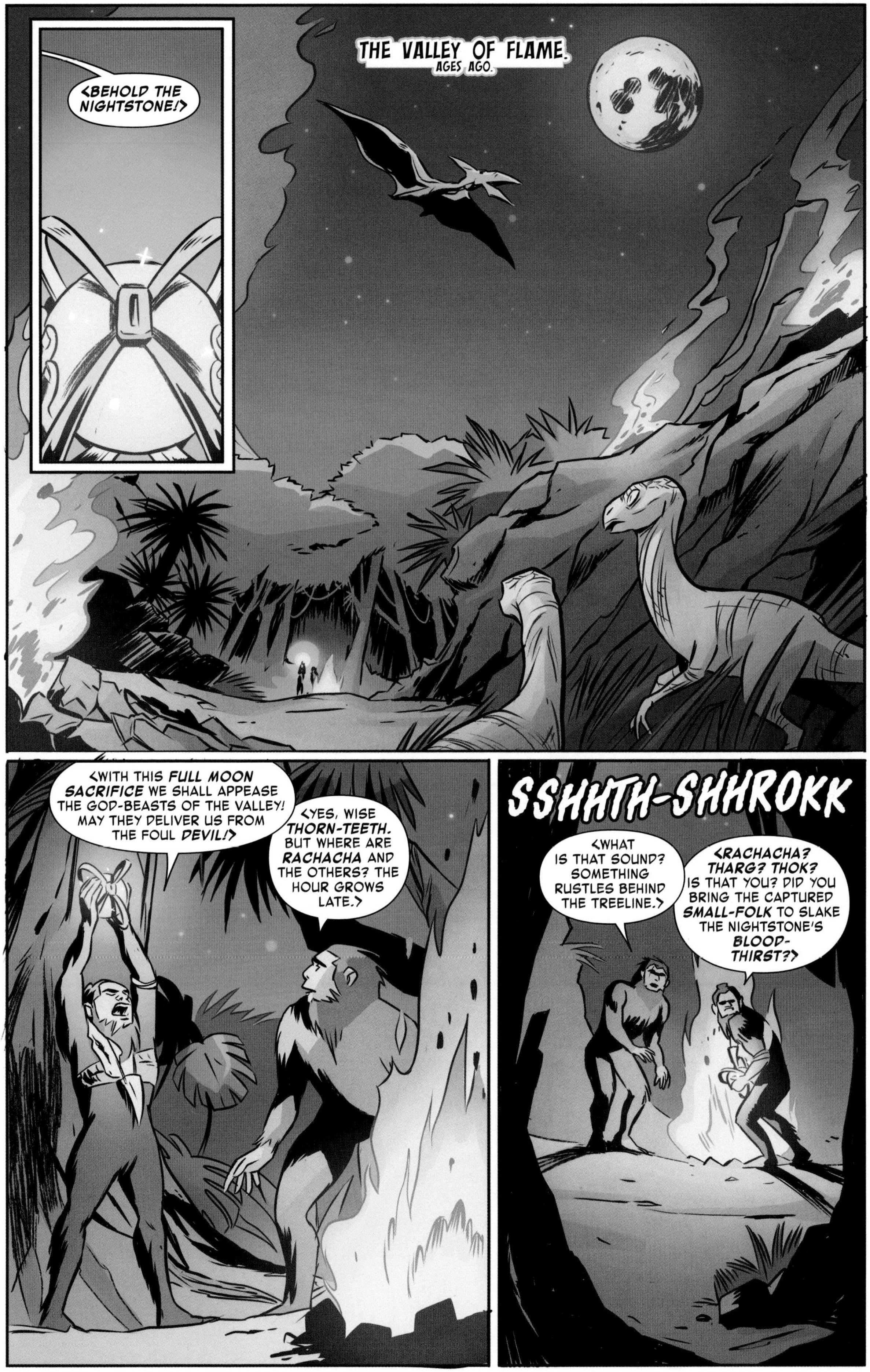

THE VALLEY OF FLAME. AGES AGO.
<BEHOLD THE NIGHTSTONE!>
<WITH THIS FULL MOON SACRIFICE WE SHALL APPEASE THE GOD-BEASTS OF THE VALLEY! MAY THEY DELIVER US FROM THE FOUL DEVIL!>
<YES, WISE THORN-TEETH. BUT WHERE ARE RACHACHA AND THE OTHERS? THE HOUR GROWS LATE.>
SSHHTH-SHHROKK
<WHAT IS THAT SOUND? SOMETHING RUSTLES BEHIND THE TREELINE.>
<RACHACHA? THARG? THOK? IS THAT YOU? DID YOU BRING THE CAPTURED SMALL-FOLK TO SLAKE THE NIGHTSTONE'S BLOOD-THIRST?>

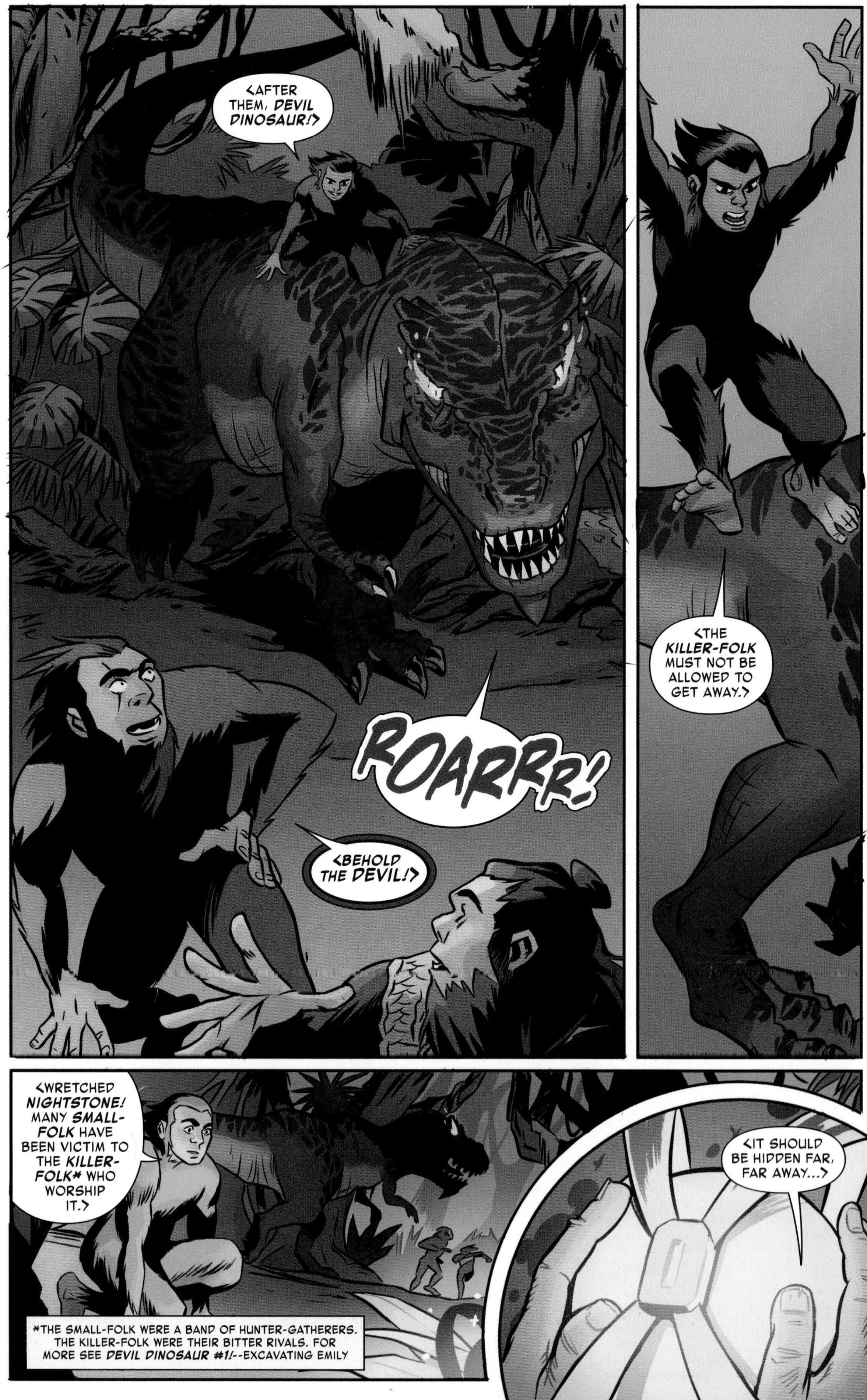
<AFTER THEM, DEVIL DINOSAUR!>
ROARRRR!
<BEHOLD THE DEVIL!>
<THE KILLER-FOLK MUST NOT BE ALLOWED TO GET AWAY.>
<WRETCHED NIGHTSTONE! MANY SMALL-FOLK HAVE BEEN VICTIM TO THE KILLER-FOLK* WHO WORSHIP IT.>
*THE SMALL-FOLK WERE A BAND OF HUNTER-GATHERERS. THE KILLER-FOLK WERE THEIR BITTER RIVALS. FOR MORE SEE DEVIL DINOSAUR #1!--EXCAVATING EMILY
<IT SHOULD BE HIDDEN FAR, FAR AWAY...>

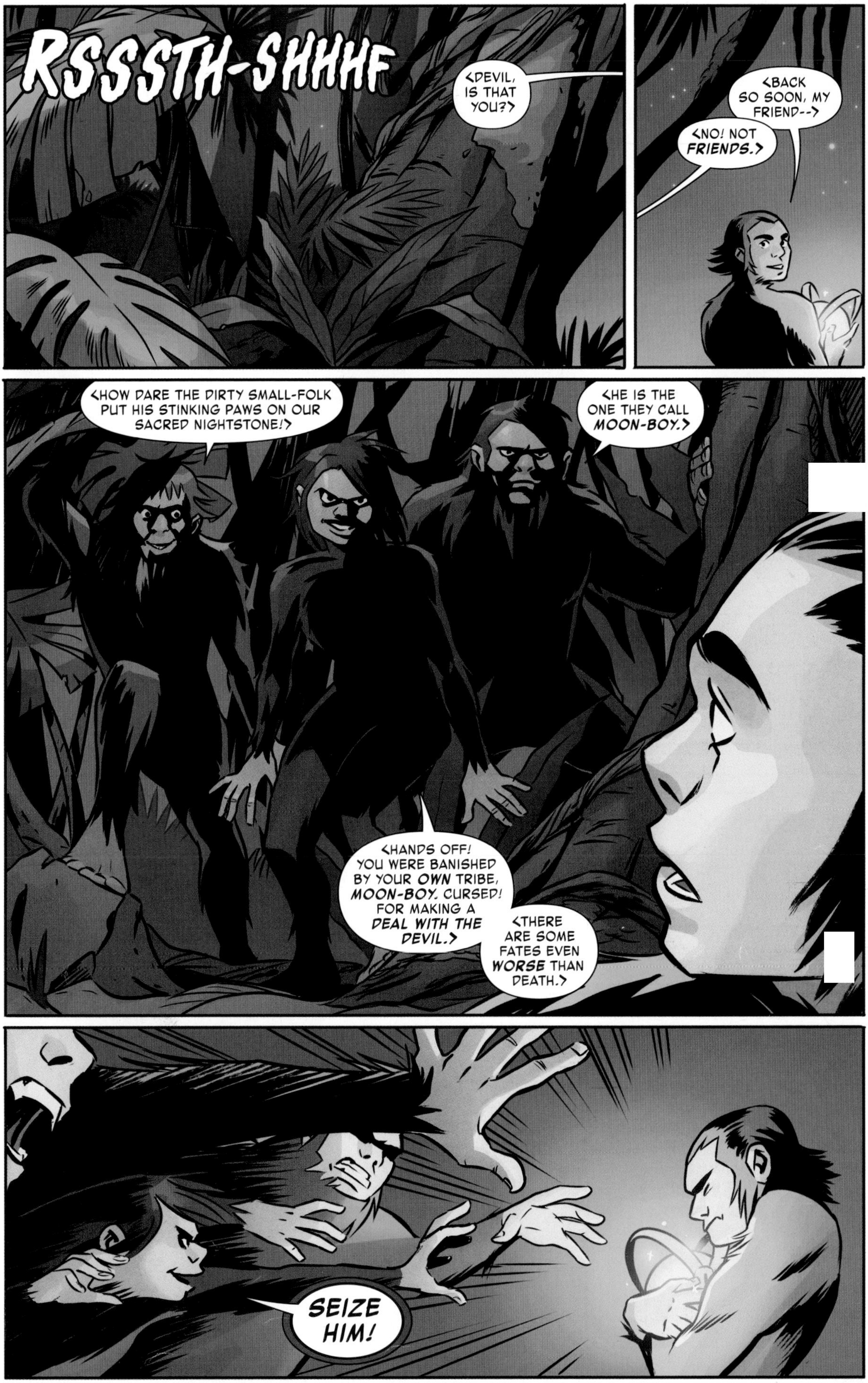
RSSSTH-SHHHF
<DEVIL, IS THAT YOU?>
<BACK SO SOON, MY FRIEND-->
<NO! NOT FRIENDS.>
<HOW DARE THE DIRTY SMALL-FOLK PUT HIS STINKING PAWS ON OUR SACRED NIGHTSTONE!>
<HE IS THE ONE THEY CALL MOON-BOY.>
<HANDS OFF! YOU WERE BANISHED BY YOUR OWN TRIBE, MOON-BOY. CURSED! FOR MAKING A DEAL WITH THE DEVIL.>
<THERE ARE SOME FATES EVEN WORSE THAN DEATH.>
SEIZE HIM!

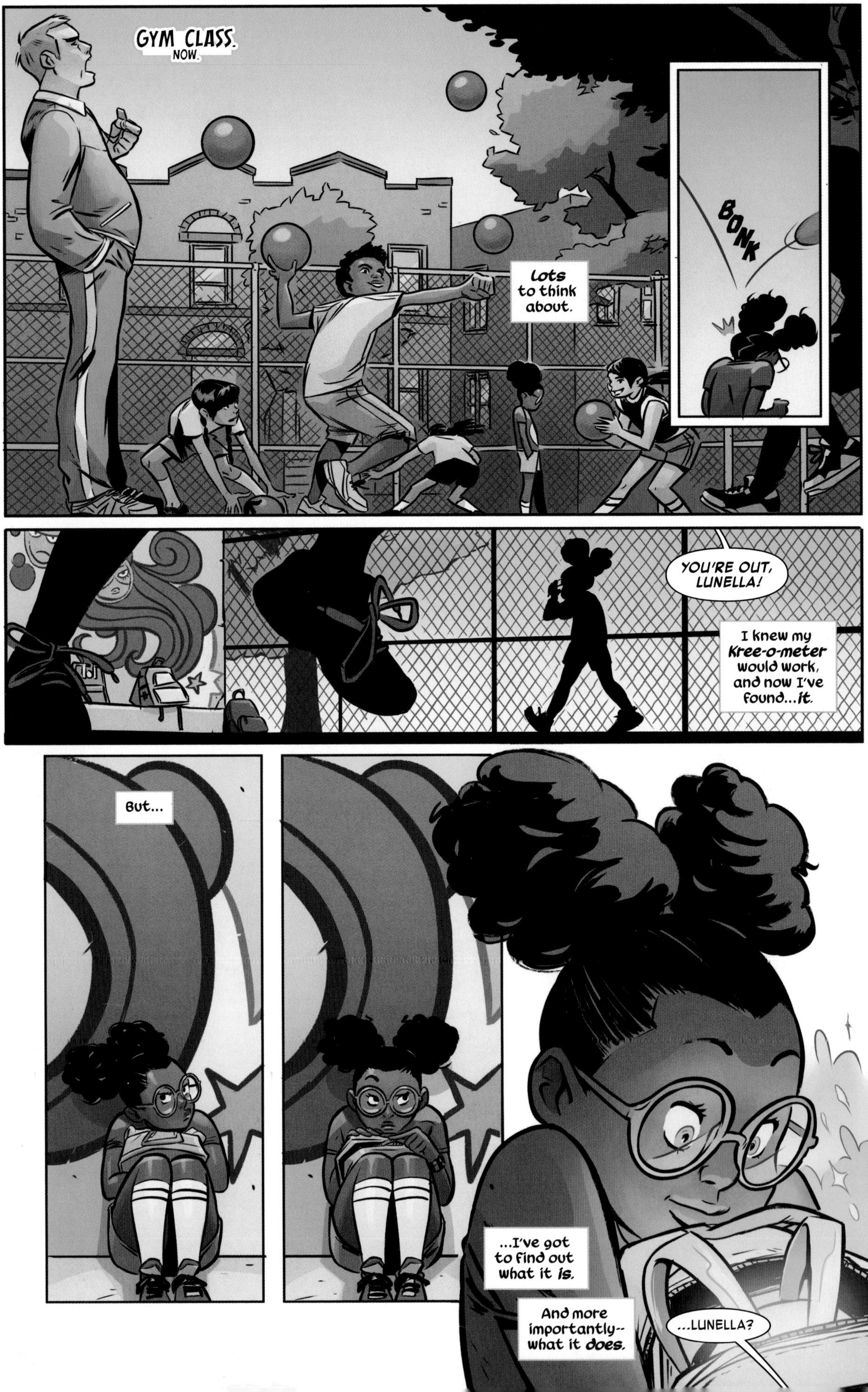
GYM CLASS.
NOW.
Lots to think about.
BONK
YOU'RE OUT, LUNELLA!
I knew my Kree-o-meter would work, and now I've found...it.
But...
...I've got to find out what it is.
And more importantly-- what it does.
...LUNELLA?

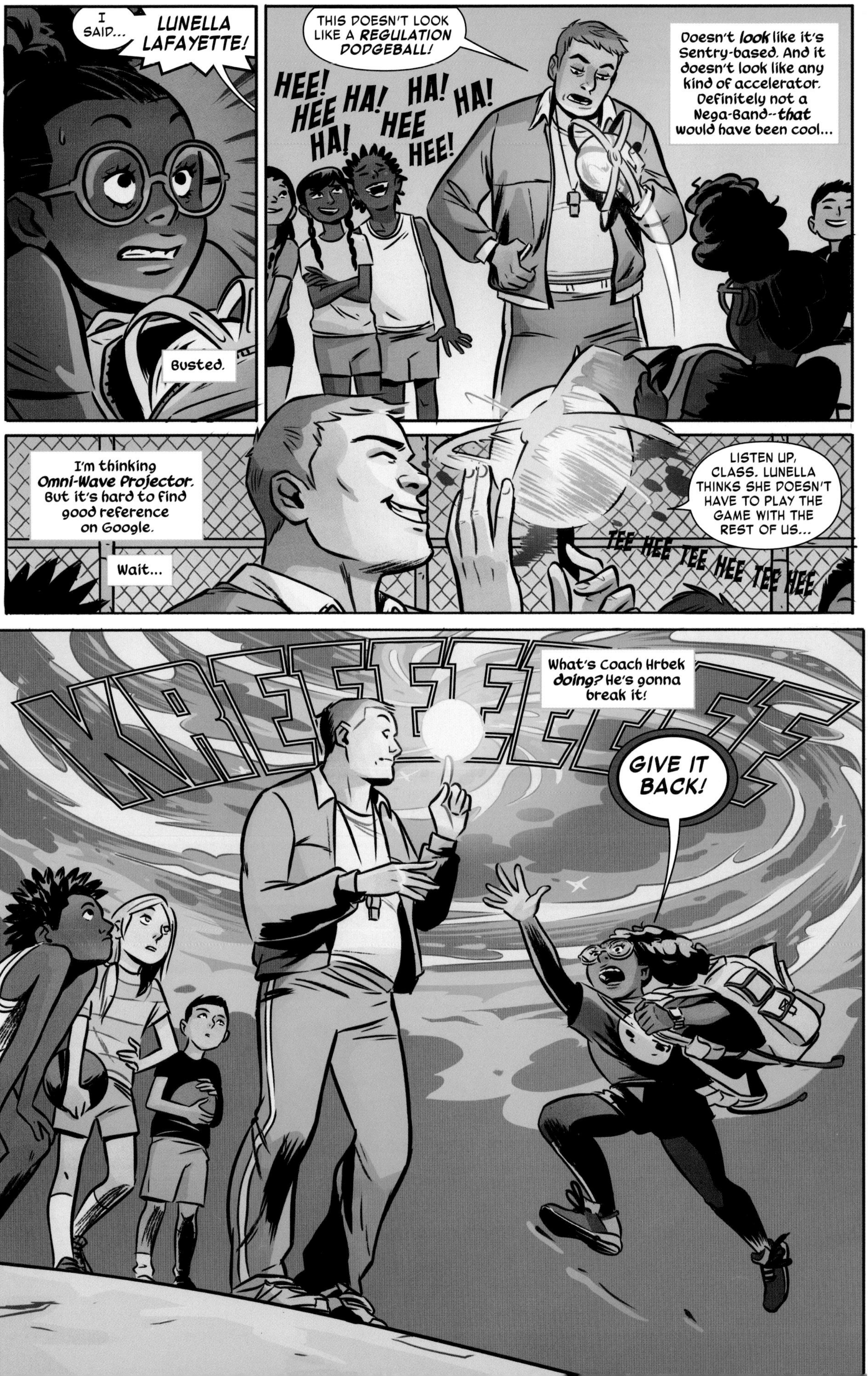
I SAID...
LUNELLA LAFAYETTE!
Busted.
THIS DOESN'T LOOK LIKE A REGULATION DODGEBALL!
HEE! HEE HA! HA! HEE HA! HEE HEE! HA!
Doesn't look like it's Sentry-based. And it doesn't look like any kind of accelerator. Definitely not a Nega-Band--that would have been cool...
I'm thinking Omni-Wave Projector. But it's hard to find good reference on Google.
Wait...
LISTEN UP, CLASS. LUNELLA THINKS SHE DOESN'T HAVE TO PLAY THE GAME WITH THE REST OF US...
TEE HEE TEE HEE TEE HEE
What's Coach Hrbek doing? He's gonna break it!
GIVE IT BACK!

THUDD THUDD THUDD THUPP

THUDD THUPP THUPP

THUDD THUDD

‹WAIT! WHAT'S HAPPENING TO THE TALISMAN?›

‹MOON-BOY HAS ANGERED THE GODS!›

KRRREEEZZZ

‹OUR NIGHTSTONE! IT'S DISAPPEARING!›

‹WE MUST GET IT BACK!›

‹RACHACHA-- THIS SORCERY DOES NOT LOOK SAFE!›

‹LOOK! A MYSTERIOUS VORTEX SWIRLS...›

‹WHO KNOWS TO WHAT STRANGE WORLD THE SMALL-FOLK SENT THE NIGHTSTONE?›

‹IT COULD BE DANGEROUS.›

‹NOW IT'LL BE MORE DANGEROUS--WHEN THE KILLER-FOLK GET THERE.›

‹LET'S FIND WHO STOLE THE NIGHTSTONE!›

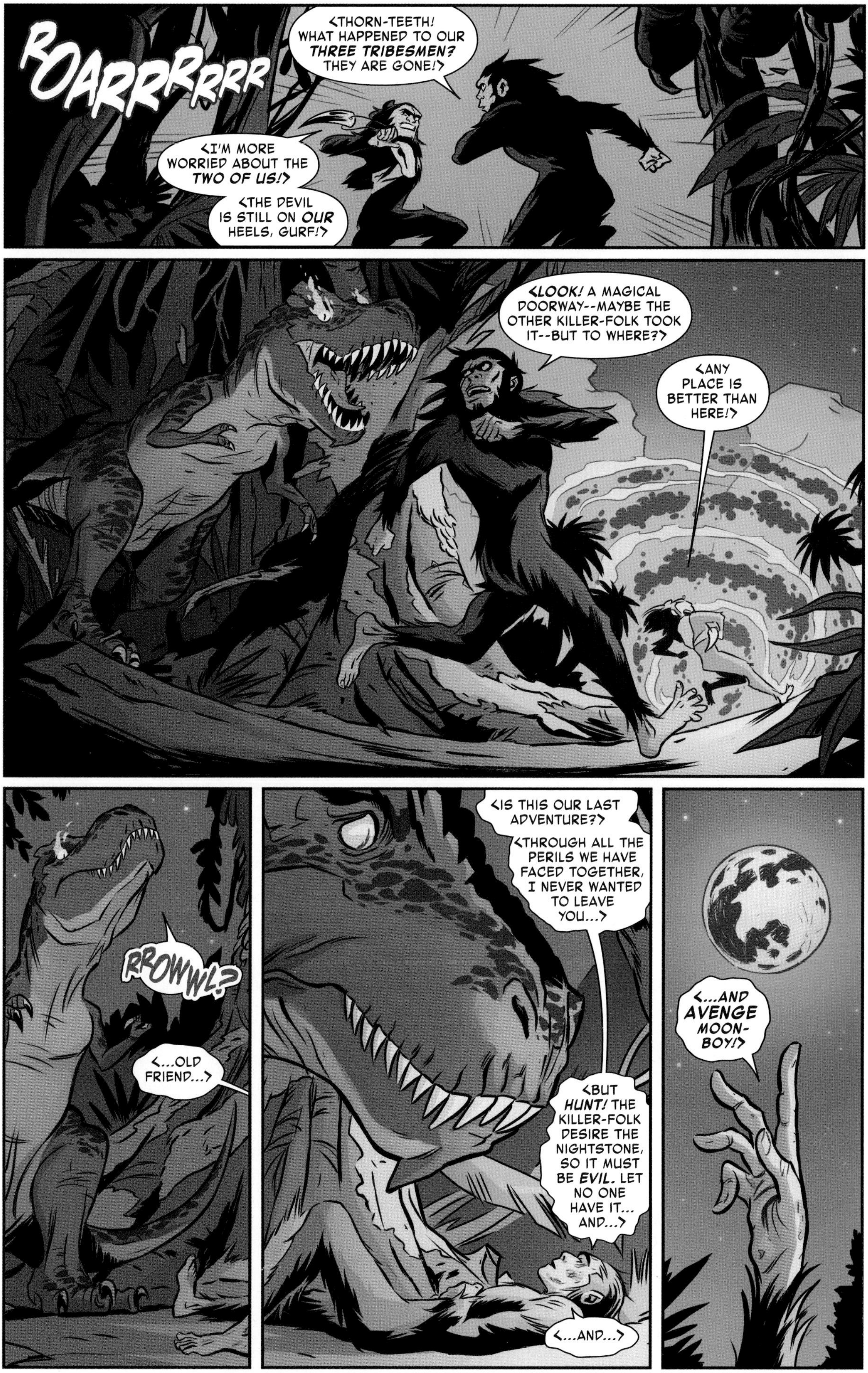

ROARRRRRRR
<THORN-TEETH! WHAT HAPPENED TO OUR THREE TRIBESMEN? THEY ARE GONE!>
<I'M MORE WORRIED ABOUT THE TWO OF US!>
<THE DEVIL IS STILL ON OUR HEELS, GURF!>
<LOOK! A MAGICAL DOORWAY--MAYBE THE OTHER KILLER-FOLK TOOK IT--BUT TO WHERE?>
<ANY PLACE IS BETTER THAN HERE!>
RROWWL?
<...OLD FRIEND...>
<IS THIS OUR LAST ADVENTURE?>
<THROUGH ALL THE PERILS WE HAVE FACED TOGETHER, I NEVER WANTED TO LEAVE YOU...>
<BUT HUNT! THE KILLER-FOLK DESIRE THE NIGHTSTONE, SO IT MUST BE EVIL. LET NO ONE HAVE IT... AND...>
<...AND...>
<...AND AVENGE MOON-BOY!>

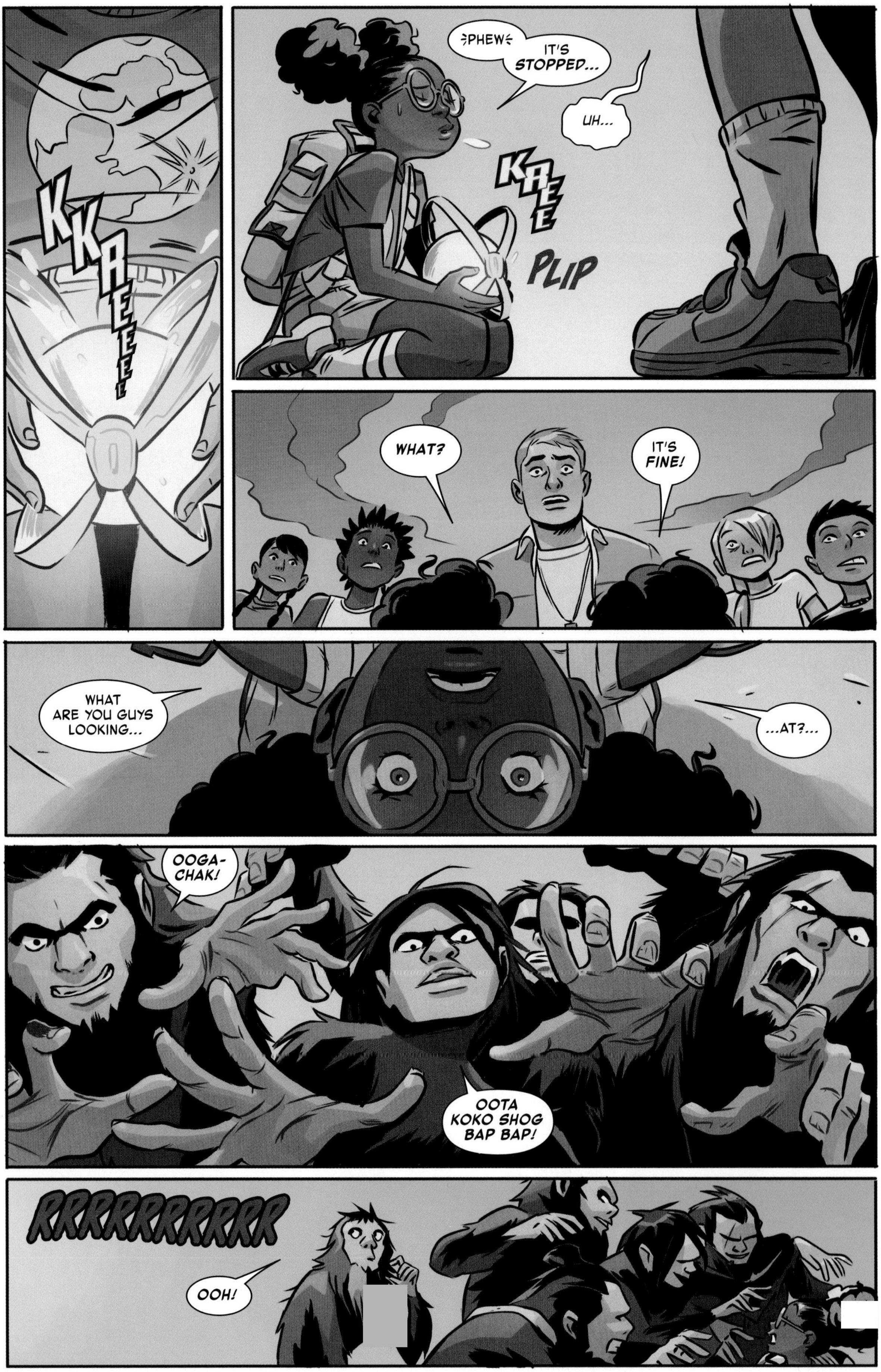
KKRAEEEEE
PHEW IT'S STOPPED...
UH...
KRAEE
PLIP
WHAT?
IT'S FINE!
WHAT ARE YOU GUYS LOOKING...
...AT?...
OOGA-CHAK!
OOTA KOKO SHOG BAP BAP!
RRRRRRRRRRR
OOH!

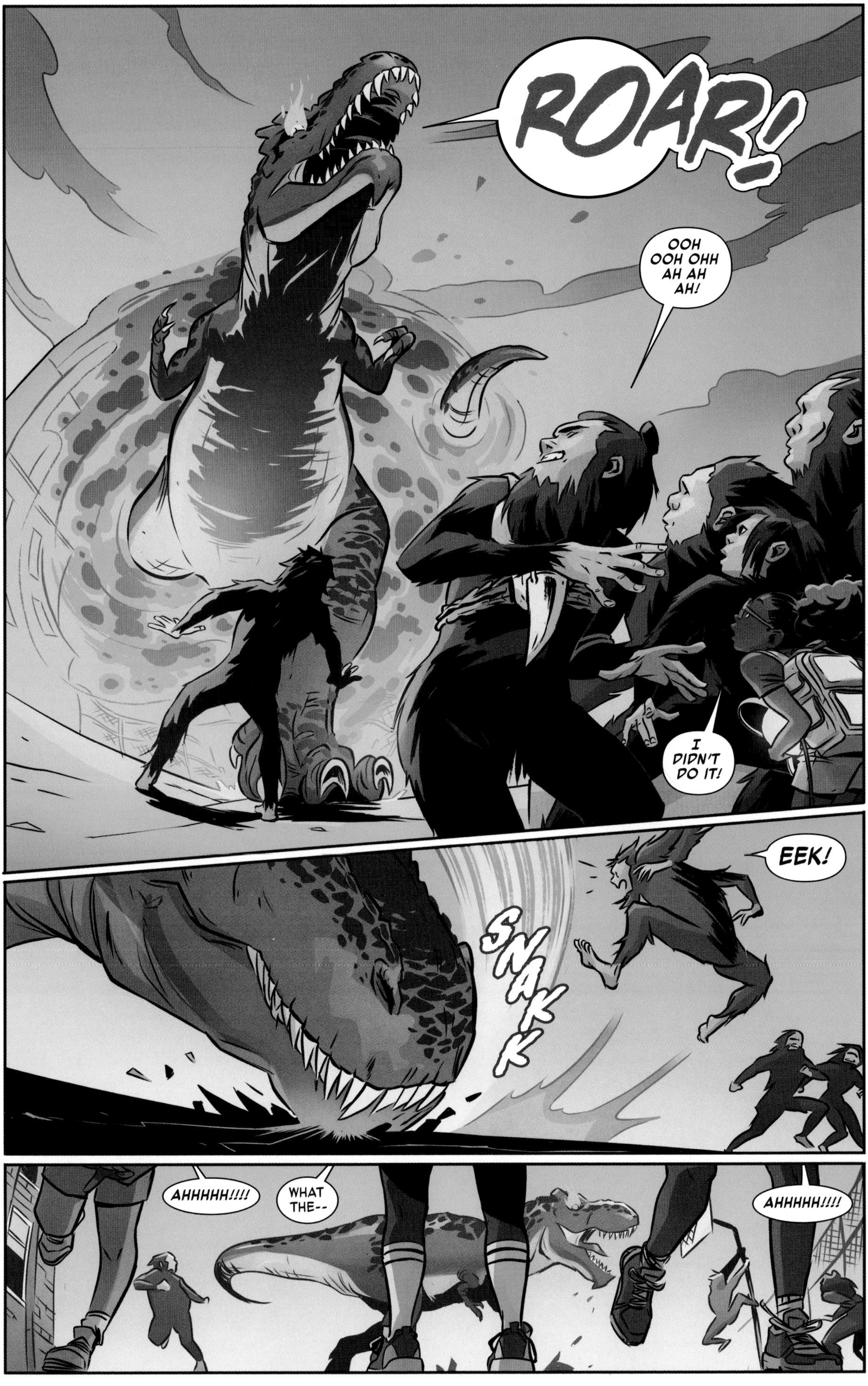
ROAR!
OOH OOH OHH AH AH AH!
I DIDN'T DO IT!
EEK!
SNAKK
AHHHHH!!!!
WHAT THE--
AHHHHH!!!!

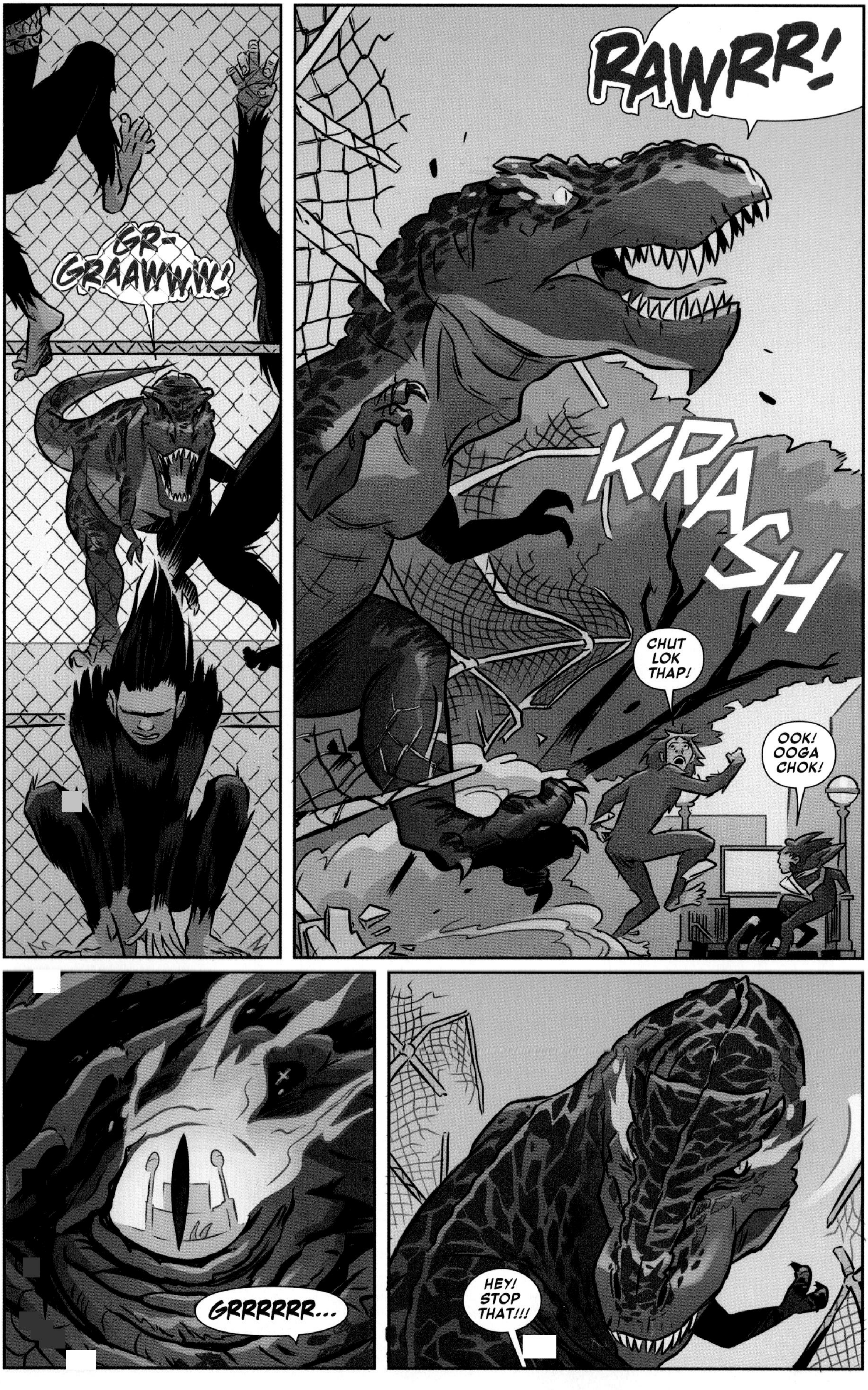
GR-GRAAWWW!
RAWRR!
KRASH
CHUT LOK THAP!
OOK! OOGA CHOK!
GRRRRRR...
HEY! STOP THAT!!!

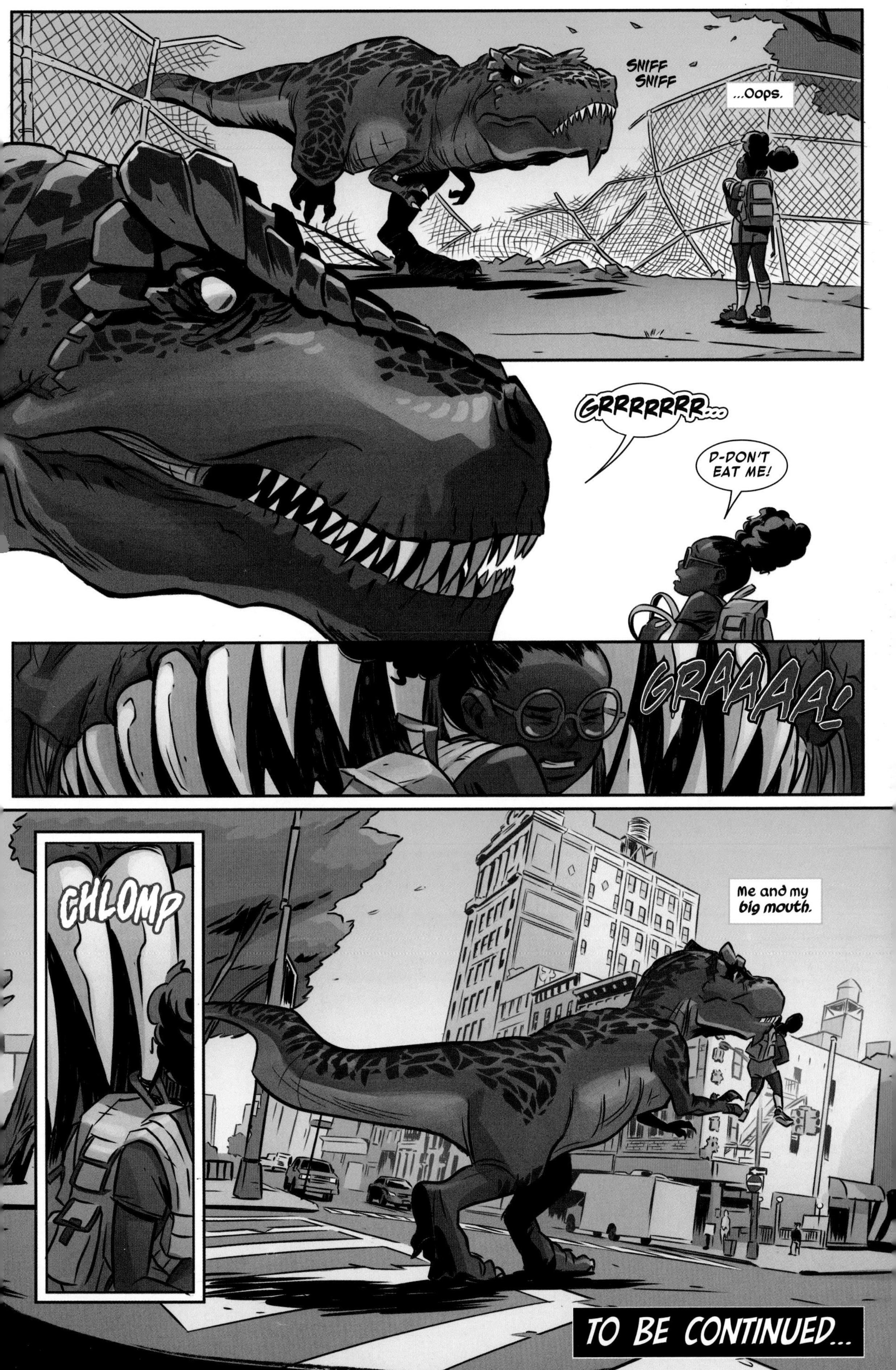
SNIFF SNIFF
...Oops.
GRRRRRRR...
D-DON'T EAT ME!
GRAAAA!
CHLOMP
Me and my big mouth.
TO BE CONTINUED...